Trouper

By **Meg Kearney** • Paintings by **E. B. Lewis**

Scholastic Press • New York

In January 2005, the "real" Trouper was picked up running with a pack of stray dogs in
the streets of Ponce, Puerto Rico. His back right leg was so mangled — probably the result
of a car accident — that it was facing in the opposite direction. The dog catcher brought
him to a "kill shelter." There, the man who was supposed to put him down was moved
deeply by this dog who — despite being in pain — was sweet, handsome, and good-tempered.
The man called a woman who ran the local shelter. "This dog is too good to put down,"
he said, and the woman came to rescue him.

    When the woman walked into the room, Trouper licked her hand, as if he knew she was
there to save him. And she brought him to a vet, who amputated his leg. Then she nursed
him back to health and listed him on her website. But month after month in the shelter,
people passed him over — until September of 2005, when Trouper found his home in
New Hampshire with Meg Kearney.

Endless gratitude from Meg Kearney to Jacqueline Woodson — for all of her encouragement and friendship over the years.
And gracious thanks to Sam Paris and to the real-life Trouper for tirelessly posing as models for this book.

E. B. Lewis would like to express his gratitude to Melissa Levy and her team of workers at PAWS (Philadelphia Animal Welfare Society),
the city's largest rescue organization and only no-kill shelter, for generously allowing him to use their spectacular dogs as models for this book.
And special thanks to Sam Paris who modeled as the boy in the story, and of course, to Trouper.

Library of Congress Cataloging-in-Publication Data

Kearney, Meg.
Trouper / by Meg Kearney ; illustrated by E. B. Lewis. — 1st ed.   p. cm.
Summary: Trouper, a three-legged dog, remembers his life as a stray, before he was adopted.
ISBN 978-0-545-10041-0 (hardcover : alk. paper) 1. Feral dogs—Juvenile fiction. 2. Dogs—Juvenile fiction.
3. Pet adoption—Juvenile fiction. [1. Novels in verse. 2. Feral dogs—Fiction. 3. Dogs—Fiction. 4. Pet adoption—Fiction.]
I. Lewis, Earl B., ill. II. Title.   PZ7.5.K43Tro 2013   813.6—dc23   2012015730

10 9 8 7 6 5 4 3 2 1   13 14 15 16 17

Printed in Malaysia   108
First edition, November 2013

The display type was set in Onyx Regular and Bradon Grotesque Black.
The text type was set in Adobe Garamond Pro.
E. B. Lewis created his illustrations with watercolor on 300 lb. Arches Cold Press paper.
Art direction and book design by Marijka Kostiw

For all the animals who are waiting to be adopted

— M. K.

To Melissa Levy and her team of workers at PAWS

— E. B. L.

Back in the before time,
before I licked your nose
or sniffed your shoes,
before you bought my bed and bowl,
before the place you picked me out,
I ran with a mob of mutts.

We tipped over trash cans,
pawing for bones;
we barked;
we howled;
we wrestled
and fought
over scraps of pizza
while dodging the stones
thrown by boys
who thought the world was mean,
and so they had to be.

Then came the windblown day
when the man wearing jeans
and a bright green cap
lured me and my mob into the back of his truck
with the biggest steak we had ever seen.
He slammed the doors and we were stuck!

Next we knew, we'd arrived at the place
filled with dogs locked in cages
and a woman who clucked
like a chicken when she saw us.
Just in case we tried to run away,
she put us in cages, too —
Hunter and Tugger, Digger, and Dice,
Big Bear and Sweet Girl, Curley, and Boo
were locked in cages and looked kind of scared.
We didn't howl or growl.
We lay down, feeling blue.

We got water and kibble
from the lady who cared for us.
We got walks,
but wished
we could race
the way we used to.

And every day,
people stared at us;
they smiled —
some glared at us
as they paced
up and down,
pointing,

then taking Hunter and Tugger

then Digger

then Dice,

then Big Bear

then Sweet Girl

then Curley —

last, Boo.

My heart was a cold, starless night —

until your face
shone through the bars
like a mini sun.
You whispered, "Good boy!"
said what a great team we'll make,
then you reached in to pet me
because you knew
I wouldn't bite.

You were skinny as a string bean
but your hand was gentle —
it would never throw stones at *me*
(maybe at a puddle or lake or tree).
If only those boys from before could have seen
how good you are.

Before you found me,
I thought all kids were mean,
though I dreamed each night
I might find just one
who didn't mind so much
my hairy stump,
who liked the way I lean on those I love.

Now we're *home*!
And here is my bowl
(it's black, like me).
Here are my bones
to chew when I want.

Here is my bed
so I can be near you
when we sleep.

But let's not sleep yet!
Let's go lie down
and eat some lunch,

then play outside —
a game called RUN —

and leave five footprints in the snow.